I AM THE
JUNGLE
A YOGA ADVENTURE

For my daughter, Penny.
May she always be happy and free.
—MH

For my siblings, with whom I explored my first jungles
on an imagined island in our New Jersey backyard.
—KT

Sounds True
Boulder, CO 80306

Text © 2020 Melissa Hurt
Illustrations © 2020 Katy Tanis

Published 2020

Book design by Ranée Kahler

Printed in South Korea

Library of Congress Cataloging-in-Publication Data

Names: Hurt, Melissa, author. | Tanis, Katy, illustrator.
Title: I am the jungle : a yoga adventure / by Melissa Hurt ; illustrated
  by Katy Tanis.
Description: Boulder, Colorado : Sounds True, 2020. | Summary: As children
  practice a sequence of yoga poses, they imagine they are the animals for
  which each pose is named, and describe the emotions each evokes.
  Includes Sanskrit names and physical benefits of each yoga pose.
Identifiers: LCCN 2019052873 (print) | LCCN 2019052874 (ebook) |
  ISBN 9781683643821 (hardback) | ISBN 9781683643838 (ebook)
Subjects: CYAC: Yoga--Fiction. | Animals--Fiction.
Classification: LCC PZ7.1.H866 Iam 2020 (print) | LCC PZ7.1.H866 (ebook) |
  DDC [E]--dc23
LC record available at https://lccn.loc.gov/2019052873
LC ebook record available at https://lccn.loc.gov/2019052874

10 9 8 7 6 5 4 3 2 1

I AM THE JUNGLE

A YOGA ADVENTURE

Melissa Hurt

Illustrated by
Katy Tanis

sounds true
BOULDER, COLORADO

Sometimes I feel like a "wild child" because I never stop running around. I just like going places! Today I'm going to the jungle.

I inhale as I sweep my arms out to the side and overhead.

I gently arch my back and gaze toward the sky . . .

I feel my feet on the ground. My breath moves my belly out and in like a gentle wave. Inhale, release, inhale, release, inhale, release.

I am a steady Mountain . . .

I balance on one foot and make a triangle with my legs. I feel grounded and free. My arms are touching the sky. I'm the tallest Tree in the jungle.

I feel the branches swishing back and forth, back and forth, back and forth . . .

I feel playful and grand as I glide through the branches. My arms spread wide and my lifted leg long like tail feathers as I swoop and dip. I'm a Turaco flying through the jungle trees.

I see the ground shaking, quaking, and quivering below me . . .

I feel powerful as I grow into a giant with my feet wide and steady on the ground. I tell the whole jungle that the Mountain Gorilla is moving through!

A loud trumpet fills the air . . .

I'm an Elephant and I love to swing my trunk from one side, back down, and to the other side up high.

In the distance, I hear a rich, rumbly roar . . .

I kneel with my head rising tall
and proud. I lean forward on my
powerful paws. I breathe
in and roar! I'm a Lion.

Ahead I sense something slide
through the grass . . .

I feel my hiss turn low and slow. Hiss, hisss, hissss . . .
I'm long and strong as I slither through the tall grasses.
I'm a Rock Python raising my head as I take in the hot
sun. My chest spreads wide and I feel mighty.

I am attracted to the cool water . . .

I sit tall and feel movement inside my long legs. I'm the Congo River flowing through the jungle.

I breathe in and reach up. I feel serene as my hands reach to my toes and then slide all the way up my legs. I gently shush the water's current.

I notice the light begins to speckle . . .

I arch my back and prop my arms close to my body with the top of my head resting on the ground. I'm a Tigerfish dashing to the surface to catch my prey.

I feel a pitter-patter in the breeze above the water's surface . . .

I feel calm and light with the bottoms of my feet together. I am a beautiful Forester Butterfly. I float and feel my wings flutter as I soar across the sky.

Overhead, I see a breezy cloud . . .

THE VERY HUNGRY CATERPILLAR

GORILLAS IN THE MIST

A Butterfly Is Patient

[waiting for Wings]

FIELD GUIDE TO AFRICAN MAMMALS

WHERE THE WILD THINGS ARE

Butterflies of the World

THE JUNGLE BOOK

THE MAGIC TREE

Tarzan of the Apes

I sit with my legs crossed and my head floating high. I'm a Cloud. I feel cool air moving through my nose and into my belly. I notice warm air leaving my nose. I am calm, happy, and free.

All of the jungle lives inside of me.

Yoga Poses in Sanskrit and Their Benefits

For the yoga sequence below, hold each pose for five breaths.
Some poses are modified to embody the animal's characteristics.
Practice each pose in its inherent form to have a more traditional practice.

**Upward Salute —
Urdhva Hastasana**
Warms up the body and
balances the mind.

Mountain Pose — Tadasana
Lengthens the spine
and provides space for
the internal organs.

Tree Pose — Vrksasana
Strengthens and stabilizes
the legs and hips.

Lion Pose — Simhasana
Opens the muscles of the face,
tongue, and throat while
releasing mental tension
through the exhalation.

Cobra Pose — Bhujangasana
Strengthens the muscles
of the middle back while
massaging the kidneys.

**Seated Forward Bend —
Paschimottanasana**
Lengthens the muscles
of the back and legs while
calming the mind.

**Half-Moon Pose —
Ardha Chandrasana**
Strengthens the muscles
in the abdomen, back,
gluteal region, and legs.

**Goddess Pose —
Utkata Konasana**
Strengthens the
legs and hips.

**Wide-Leg Forward Fold —
Prasarita Padottanasana**
Lengthens the muscles
in the back and legs.

Fish Pose — Matsyasana
Lengthens the muscles in the
belly and throat. Strengthens
the muscles in the upper
back and neck.

**Bound Angle Pose —
Baddha Konasana**
Opens the hips
and inner legs.

Easy Pose — Sukhasana
Relaxes the
body and mind.